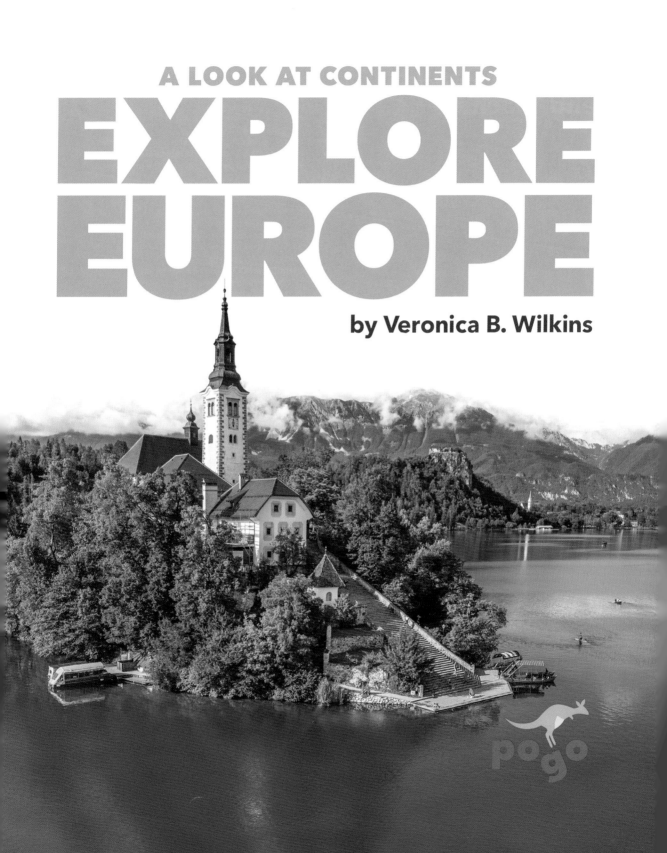

A LOOK AT CONTINENTS
EXPLORE EUROPE

by Veronica B. Wilkins

pogo

Ideas for Parents and Teachers

Pogo Books let children practice reading informational text while introducing them to nonfiction features such as headings, labels, sidebars, maps, and diagrams, as well as a table of contents, glossary, and index.

Carefully leveled text with a strong photo match offers early fluent readers the support they need to succeed.

Before Reading

• "Walk" through the book and point out the various nonfiction features. Ask the student what purpose each feature serves.

• Look at the glossary together. Read and discuss the words.

Read the Book

• Have the child read the book independently.

• Invite him or her to list questions that arise from reading.

After Reading

• Discuss the child's questions. Talk about how he or she might find answers to those questions.

• Prompt the child to think more. Ask: What did you know about Europe before reading this book? Would you like to learn more?

Pogo Books are published by Jump!
5357 Penn Avenue South
Minneapolis, MN 55419
www.jumplibrary.com

Library of Congress Cataloging-in-Publication Data

Names: Names: Wilkins, Veronica B., 1994- author.
Title: Explore Europe / by Veronica B. Wilkins.
Description: Minneapolis, MN: Jump!, [2020]
Series: A look at continents
Audience: Ages: 7-10
Identifiers: LCCN 2019036540 (print)
LCCN 2019036541 (ebook)
ISBN 9781645272946 (hardcover)
ISBN 9781645272953 (paperback)
ISBN 9781645272960 (ebook)
Subjects: LCSH: Europe—Geography—Juvenile literature. | Europe—Population—Juvenile literature.
Classification: LCC D900 .W55 2020 (print)
LCC D900 (ebook) | DDC 940—dc23
LC record available at https://lccn.loc.gov/2019036540
LC ebook record available at https://lccn.loc.gov/2019036541

Editor: Susanne Bushman
Designer: Anna Peterson

Photo Credits: Rastislav Sedlak SK/Shutterstock, cover; ZGPhotography/Shutterstock, 1; Shaiith/Shutterstock, 3; Eye Ubiquitous/SuperStock, 4; Photopat iceland/Alamy, 5; Maciej Es/Shutterstock, 6-7 (foreground); Jaroslav74/Shutterstock, 6-7 (background); rayints/Shutterstock, 8-9; Skouatroulio/iStock, 10-11; Hans Blossey/Getty, 12-13; Dmitry Chulov/Shutterstock, 14; Mark Medcalf/Shutterstock, 15; UA-pro/Shutterstock, 16-17; Viacheslav Lopatin/Shutterstock, 18; Memitina/Getty, 19; LightField Studios/Shutterstock, 20-21 (foreground); jeafish Ping/Shutterstock, 20-21 (background); Myroslava Bozhko/Shutterstock, 23.

Printed in the United States of America at Corporate Graphics in North Mankato, Minnesota.

TABLE OF CONTENTS

CHAPTER 1

A LONG COAST

Let's explore the **continent** of Europe! Mount Etna is here. It is one of the most active **volcanoes** in the world.

Mount Etna ····▶

Iceland is a country in Europe. It has more **hot springs** than any other country on Earth. People swim and relax in these warm pools!

Europe is the second smallest continent. It is north of the **equator**. It is in the Northern **Hemisphere**. It is connected to Asia in the east. The Mediterranean Sea separates it from Africa.

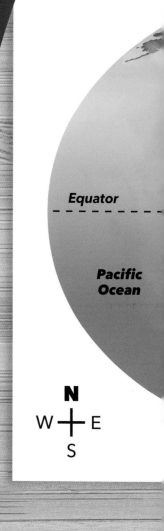

Equator

Pacific Ocean

N
W E
S

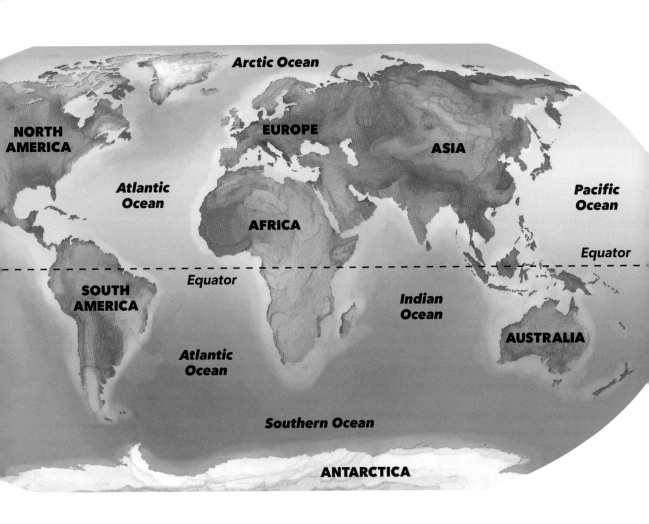

Arctic Ocean

EUROPE

ASIA

NORTH
AMERICA

Atlantic
Ocean

Pacific
Ocean

AFRICA

Equator

Equator

SOUTH
AMERICA

Indian
Ocean

Atlantic
Ocean

AUSTRALIA

Southern Ocean

ANTARCTICA

Norwegian fjords

This continent has many **peninsulas**. It has around 24,000 miles (38,624 kilometers) of coastline. **Fjords** line the coast in the north. The coast of the Iberian Peninsula in the south has warm beaches. Many are surrounded by cliffs.

DID YOU KNOW?

Fjords were made by **glaciers**. How? These large sheets of ice moved from higher land to the sea. They carved deep valleys into the land. These valleys filled with water to become fjords.

The Ural Mountains are east. They divide Europe from Asia. The Alps are mountains. They cross the center of Europe. Europe's highest peak is here. Matterhorn is 14,692 feet (4,478 meters) high.

Matterhorn

Danube
River

Many rivers cross this continent. The Volga River is the longest. It is around 2,200 miles (3,541 km) long. The Danube River passes through 10 countries.

The Pripet River creates around 104,000 square miles (269,359 square km) of **wetlands**. They are home to many animals.

WHAT DO YOU THINK?

Most cities in Europe form near or around bodies of water. Why do you think this is?

CHAPTER 2

WILDLIFE AND CLIMATES

The northern part of this continent is **polar**. Snowy owls live here. Caribou roam. They **migrate** south in winter.

Animals of the Alps have special features to live in the mountains. Like what? Some rabbits and birds turn white in winter. Why? They can hide better in the snow!

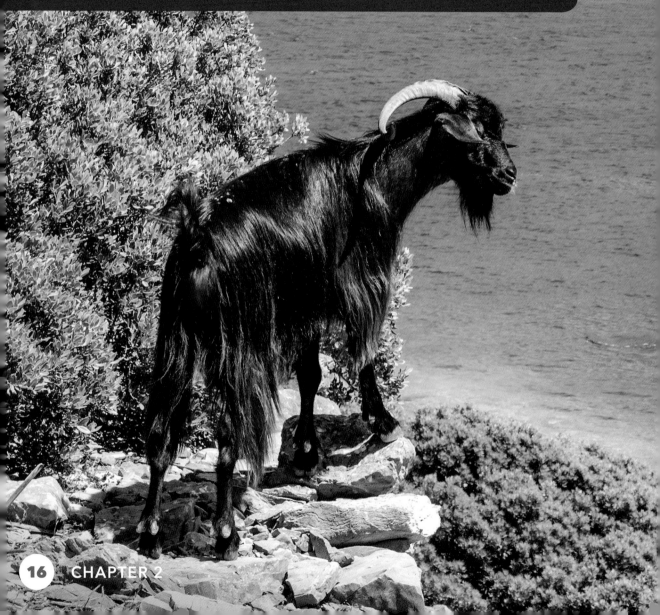

The **climate** here is mostly **temperate**. The south is warm. This **region** is called the Mediterranean. Why? It is by the Mediterranean Sea. Wild goats and sheep live in the mountains and woods here.

TAKE A LOOK!

What are the climate regions of Europe? Take a look!

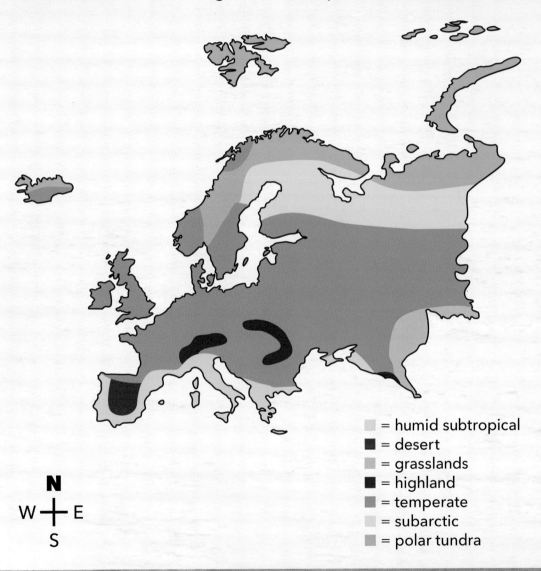

N
W + E
S

= humid subtropical
= desert
= grasslands
= highland
= temperate
= subarctic
= polar tundra

CHAPTER 3

LIFE IN EUROPE

Most people here live in cities. Athens is one of the oldest. Many very old buildings fill the city.

Athens, Greece

London is a city in the United Kingdom. It is home to more than eight million people. Markets here sell food from around the world.

There are around 160 **cultural** groups here. Many languages are spoken. Children often learn other languages in school.

Europe is full of amazing sights! Would you like to explore it?

WHAT DO YOU THINK?

Many countries in Europe formed a group. It is called the European Union. The union makes it easier to move between countries. Would you like to move to a new country? Why or why not?

EU

QUICK FACTS & TOOLS

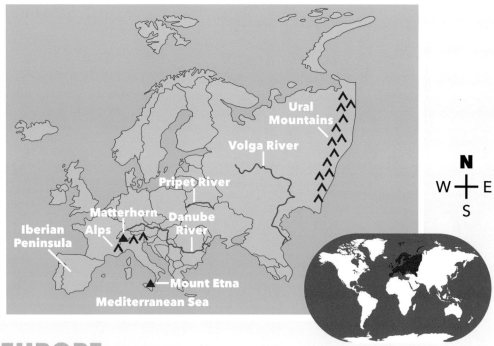

Ural Mountains

Volga River

Pripet River

Matterhorn

Alps

Danube River

Iberian Peninsula

Mount Etna

Mediterranean Sea

N W E S

EUROPE

Size: 3,930,000 square miles (10,178,653 square km)

Size Rank: Asia, Africa, North America, South America, Antarctica, **Europe**, Australia

Population Estimate: 750 million (2019 estimate)

Exports: machine tools, automobiles, aircraft, chemicals

Facts: Europe makes up about 7 percent of Earth's land.

Europe is slightly larger than the United States.

climate: The weather typical of a certain place over a long period of time.

continent: One of the seven large landmasses of Earth.

cultural: Of or relating to the ideas, customs, traditions, and ways of life of a group of people.

equator: An imaginary line around the middle of Earth that is an equal distance from the North and South Poles.

fjords: Long, narrow inlets of the ocean between high cliffs.

glaciers: Very large, slow-moving masses of ice.

hemisphere: Half of a round object, especially of Earth.

hot springs: Sources of hot water that flow naturally from the ground.

migrate: To move from one region or habitat to another.

peninsulas: Pieces of land that stick out from a larger landmass and are almost completely surrounded by water.

polar: Near or having to do with the icy regions around the North or South Poles.

region: A general area or a specific district or territory.

temperate: A climate that rarely has very high or very low temperatures.

volcanoes: Mountains with openings through which molten lava, ash, and hot gases erupt, sometimes violently.

wetlands: Areas where there is a lot of moisture in the soil.

INDEX

TO LEARN MORE

Finding more information is as easy as 1, 2, 3.

1 **Go to www.factsurfer.com**

2 **Enter "exploreEurope" into the search box.**

3 **Choose your book to see a list of websites.**

FACT SURFER